About the Author

Xavier Drogon writes and tells fantasy stories to his friend, the faerie. He is married, lives in a castle, and has a dragon as a pet.

Black Fang's Dungeon

Xavier Drogon

Black Fang's Dungeon

Olympia Publishers
London

www.olympiapublishers.com
OLYMPIA PAPERBACK EDITION

Copyright © Xavier Drogon 2024

The right of Xavier Drogon to be identified as author of
this work has been asserted in accordance with sections 77 and 78 of
the Copyright, Designs and Patents Act 1988.

All Rights Reserved

No reproduction, copy or transmission of this publication
may be made without written permission.
No paragraph of this publication may be reproduced,
copied or transmitted save with the written permission of the publisher,
or in accordance with the provisions
of the Copyright Act 1956 (as amended).

Any person who commits any unauthorised act in relation to
this publication may be liable to criminal
prosecution and civil claims for damage.

A CIP catalogue record for this title is
available from the British Library.

ISBN: 978-1-83543-072-9

This is a work of fiction.
Names, characters, places and incidents originate from the writer's
imagination. Any resemblance to actual persons, living or dead, is
purely coincidental.

First Published in 2024

Olympia Publishers
Tallis House
2 Tallis Street
London
EC4Y 0AB

Printed in Great Britain

Prologue
Skeletons King's Crypt

Eustice hailed from the town of Sandpoint in a land called Varisia on the coast of the great Steaming Sea. Life in the small town is simple but also hard – the surrounding wilderness is full of goblins and other monsters.

The town of Sandpoint has over a thousand citizens calling it home – which most are human, there are a few elves and dwarves thrown in the mix. Sandpoint is a rustic and prosperous town even though it had to deal with several disasters in the past five decades, which weathered those trials and emerged stronger after each one. It hosts several thriving industries, which include lumber, fishing, farming, and glassblowing, as well as several unique businesses and entertainment venues.

There are a few notable people within the town, such as the mayor who is, Kendra Deverin, who is friendly and approachable, Ameiko Kaijitsu, who owns the tavern and inn called the Rusty Dragon; and an elf huntress Shalelu, who patrols the Sandpoint hinterlands keeping an eye on the roads looking out for goblins who terrorise the common folk from time to time.

Eustice became an accomplished warrior when he dispatched a couple of goblins in the heat of battle with them. Those two creatures were wreaking havoc on the roadway not far from Sandpoint.

Just as Eustice cut down the second of the goblins, Shalelu came upon the aftermath and congratulated him for his efforts of keeping the roadway safe and then informed him that the mayor was looking for someone to take on a job of sorts.

"Does it pay well?"

"I would believe so, yes," she said.

"What about them?" Eustice pointed to the dead goblins when he asked that question.

"I'll take care of them. You best get to the mayor as soon as possible before someone else takes that job."

Eustice accepted the invitation and sought an audience with Kendra Deverin, and upon talking with her, she said that some of the goblins in the area have been growing a lot bolder than usual, carrying off children and livestock from outlying farmsteads and would offer compensation for clearing out a nearby dungeon where some have been said to live.

Still wearing his sturdy suit of chainmail and his father's old long sword strapped to his side, he headed off into the woods, following the crude map the mayor had given him. After several hours of travelling on foot, Eustice arrived at a desolate hillside and just up ahead was a dark entrance to a tunnel leading deep underground.

He gathered up his courage and headed inside, and found himself in a dark, dusty passage heading down into the earth. As he traversed deeper underground, the light from the entrance quickly faded to no more than a faint glow, which he was forced to use a torch to light his way.

From its flickering light, Eustice saw that the tunnel opened into a room just up ahead, and he heard a quiet growl, which prompted him to draw his sword from its sheath. Suddenly, he detected movement as a pile of rags in the corner leapt up, revealing itself to be a vile goblin with warty green skin and a head shaped like a watermelon. Its filthy clothes were covered in bloodstains, and in one hand, it still held a roasted leg of a stolen sheep, and in the other hand was a wicked-looking short sword. The creature snarled at Eustice and charged, dropping its meal on the ground.

With a desperate lunge, Eustice slid past the goblin's guard and sent his blade plunging into its chest. The goblin snarled one last time in pain and frustration, then its bulbous eyes closed, and it slumped to the ground, dead. The young warrior looked through a filthy pouch on the creatures' belt and found seven gold pieces and a small glass vial filled with red liquid. Determining that the liquid was a potion of healing, he pocketed the vial for later use, as well as the gold coins.

Eustice looked around the chamber and saw the rest was empty, but there were two corridors that led deeper into the earth. He noticed that the east corridor was full of cobwebs and looked like it had not been used in a long time. The west corridor smelt of hay and mould but was clear of webs. Considering his options, Eustice chose the passage that was free of cobwebs as he was more apt to deal with the known instead of the unknown therefore, he continued his journey.

The smell of mould grew stronger with each step down the western corridor. After so many feet, Eustice came upon a wooden door that was standing half opened, revealing a room beyond. In the room, he saw a large cage made up of iron bars with a layer of mouldy hay in the bottom, and lying in the hay was a farm boy who was from Sandpoint, one of the children who went missing in a recent goblin attack. The boy looked hungry and was covered with bruises. Eustice also noticed a large key dangling from a hook a few feet off the floor across the room from the cage. When he looked back at the boy, he appeared to be fast asleep.

Thinking that the key might fit the lock on the farm boy's cage, Eustice took it from the hook and called out to the boy, and the boy's eyes slowly opened. "Thank the gods!" the boy croaked through cracked and bloodied lips. "I was out working the fields when that goblin ambushed me. I think he's going to eat me. Please let me out of here! I just want to go home."

"Don't worry, kid, I'll get you out, and don't worry about that foul creature any more. It just had its last meal."

"Thank you!" the farm boy sobbed as Eustice opened the door of the cage. "I've been trapped here for days. I'm getting out of here, but if you're going to keep going, you should be careful. There's something far more terrible than a goblin deeper in the dungeon – the goblin called it the Skeleton King. Here, take my mace with you."

The boy brushed aside some of the straw on the cell floor and pulled out a weapon that looked like a club with a large metal head.

"I managed to hide it down the back of my shirt when the goblin captured me. I think you're going to need it against whatever's hiding down there. Good luck!" With that, the young boy raced out of the dungeon, heading home to his family and safety.

With nothing left to do in the chamber, he was in, sheathing his long sword in favour of the new weapon, Eustice turned from the room, heading back up the passageway to the chamber with the dead goblin and the only way left to go was the eastern corridor with the cobwebs.

Using his torch to burn away the webs, he carefully made his way down the passage, and after a few feet, the corridor turned to the south and proceeded a few more feet before opening into a large chamber.

The large chamber was mostly empty except for the cobwebs

hanging from the ceiling. Across the room, he saw a gruesome stone sculpture of a devil perched above an open doorway. Scattered across the floor were a few gold coins. Through the doorway, Eustice saw a flight of stairs going down deeper into the earth.

Seeing no monsters in the large chamber, he made his way towards the stairs, stopping to pick up the coins along the way. About halfway through the chamber, his foot had caught on a hidden tripwire, and suddenly, a blast of flame shot out of the stone devil's mouth and was coming straight towards him.

With no time to waste, Eustice leapt back out of the room before the flame engulfed him completely. Unfortunately, he didn't fully escape the onslaught and only got minor burns but still survived the trap. He then continued collecting the coins, pocketing them, and all that remained was the scorched statue and the staircase leading down. Knowing that it was going to get more dangerous the deeper he went, Eustice continued his course.

The ancient stone stairs were slick with moisture as he descended further underground, and when he reached the bottom, he found himself in a large natural cavern filled with stalactites and stalagmites. He saw shallow pools of water on the floor and a large crack in the far wall that looked like a passageway.

As he was crossing the chamber, something didn't seem quite right to him, so he stopped in his tracks and looked around. Although he couldn't shake the weird feeling that something's wrong, he just chalked it up to nerves and continued onward. As he resumed his walking, however, his boot came down on a nondescript patch of yellow mould that was growing on the stone. Suddenly, there was a giant whooshing sound, and the air around him exploded into a cloud of yellow spores that seemed to be everywhere at once, filling his mouth and nose.

Those spores caused Eustice to cough and choke, making his eyes water and his arms feel weak. When the spores had settled, he was able to see again through yellow-tinged tears.

He made his way to the crack in the back of the chamber, where he found that it was indeed a passageway. There was a flickering of light that beckoned up ahead, accompanied by the rattle of dry bones. The passageway ended in a huge chamber with an arched ceiling. Stairs on the far side of the room led up to a small platform, and atop loomed a golden throne decorated with glittering diamonds and rubies.

There, sitting on the throne, was a skeleton dressed in the ancient and rusted armour of a king, clasped in its bony hands was a weirdly glowing long sword. Suddenly, the skeleton's head turned towards Eustice, its empty eye sockets filled with red flames. The thing's jaw opened in a horrible smile as it raised the long sword and pointed it at the young man.

"So," it rasped in a voice like two stones scraping together. "Your pitiful town has sent a champion. How kind of them. Since you've clearly slain my goblin servant, it's only fair that you take his place and join me – in death."

With a grating laugh, the skeleton stood up and moved towards the warrior, reading its long sword to attack.

"No, I wouldn't call myself a champion; this is my first time doing this kind of work. Now it's time to teach you a lesson, I hope."

Still feeling a little weak and sickly from those spores entering his system, the first three swings of the mace never did connect with the intended target, but Eustice was able to dodge the first two blows of the blade of the long sword the skeleton wielded.

Eustice then felt a sting in his non-sword arm as the undead slashed him its third strike and left a gash with blood trickling out of the cut. The valiant warrior did manage to land a blow in the thing's torso on the fourth attempt, but the skeleton didn't crumble as Eustice thought it would, but it fought on, striking the young warrior in the chest, slashing through the chainmail he wore but was still able to fight on.

With one last swing of the mace, the skeleton's bones cracked and crumbled. Bones and armour fell to the floor like a puppet with its strings cut, and as Eustice watched, the ancient corpse began to crumble to dust and rust until only the softly glowing long sword remained. He had finally defeated the undead lord of the crypt.

Eustice looked around the skeleton king's throne room and decided to take the magical long sword and pry four diamonds and six rubies from the throne itself before leaving the place for good and heading back to town, all the while drinking the potion to regain his health.

The townsfolk cheered as he strode through the streets with the skeleton's glowing long sword slung at his hip. From the front steps of the town hall, he regaled the mayor and the townspeople with the tale of his victory, after which she presented him with his reward: a bulging sack containing one hundred gold coins – which was more money than he had seen in his entire life. A local merchant offered to buy the diamonds and the rubies for a hefty sum.

With the gold from the mayor's reward and selling the gems, he had more than enough money to buy better armour and perhaps other items like a magic potion or two.

At that time, Eustice had been thinking that maybe the life of a heroic adventurer might hold a lot of promise. So thus, the adventures of Eustice began.

Chapter 1

Eustice hometown of Sandpoint is a quaint seaside settlement that periodically has problems with monsters, such as wicked goblins and hungry ghouls, but the citizens always manage to endure and survive. Lately, however, a far greater danger had come to threaten the town.

    Some weeks ago, livestock started to disappear from nearby farms. Sometimes, a half-eaten corpse was found, sometimes only bloodstains. The people of Sandpoint were afraid, and the mayor, Kendra Deverin, was growing desperate. She hoped some heroes would volunteer to search out the menace and put an end to it before it killed a person. She'd offered a reward of substantial amount to the group that stopped the mysterious creature. Although no one had seen the killer directly, a long black fang was found in one of the animal corpses, prompting the locals to dub the unseen killer 'Black Fang.'

    Eustice had heard the latest news and rumours of the recent events while in the Rusty Dragon by patrons who stopped by to quench their thirst from their long travels and the local townsfolk who heard the news from outlying farmers. He was a little dumbfounded as he thought he had taken care of that problem of the livestock disappearing along with the children from the farmsteads. But upon hearing about the long fang being found and this new greater threat, he was wrong in his assumptions.

    He heard a group talking amongst themselves while he sat at the bar as their table was right behind him. They were talking about the increase in goblin activity as well as the farm animals being eaten. They had mentioned being waylaid by a small band of goblins on the road while coming to Sandpoint. They discussed the reward the mayor was offering and was deciding on heading out to stop the creature and help the locals in ridding the menace from the land.

The barmaid told them that a group had already left some time ago, but their fates were unknown now. One of them in the group asked her if she heard about where this 'Black Fang' may be located, and she told them that she had heard that the creature may be found in a cave just south of Nettlewood.

Upon hearing the question being asked of where Nettlewood was at, Eustice turned around and said, "I know where that is. I can show you."

"You do? Who might you be my friend," an older man in the group queried.

"This is Eustice. He saved a local boy recently. There were children going missing some time ago," the barmaid said.

"Well, yes. I grew up in these lands and travelled with my father when I was younger. I know where a lot of places are and quite good with a sword," Eustice said.

"Then we must go soon," said the young woman wearing clerics garbs.

"The sooner, the better," said the roguelike, an elven female.

"But first, another round of ale," said the young warrior.

It wasn't long before the group set out of the town of Sandpoint for their destination. Along the way, Eustice learned much about his companions.

Chapter 2

As they travelled on Lost Coast Road from Sandpoint, the four who followed Eustice were Valeros, Ezren, Kyra, and Merisiel.

Valeros was supposed to have gotten married, but not wanting to be tied down to one place, he left with a change of clothes, some food, and an axe handle for a weapon. He fell in with a group of mercenaries for a while, but not wanting to work for cheats, swindlers, and cruel men, he took matters into his own hands and got out on his own and fell into the group he's with now.

Ezren is a son of a successful spice merchant which he enjoyed the comforts of a well-to-do family. He lived in a neighbourhood safe from crime and had no lofty ambitions, however, the church of the merchant god accused his father of heresy and corruption, ruining the family business. To Ezrens shock, the accusations were true. He left his home and began studying magick on his own, as no wizard would take on a forty-year-old as an apprentice. He travelled the world and fell into the group he's with now.

Kyra became a Priestess of Sarenrae, the healer sun goddess who destroys evil. She grew up admiring the beautiful stained glass of Sarenrae's temple and the graceful priestesses who practiced with their scimitars each dawn. When bandits attacked her village, those priestesses fought to the death, but the bandits were too many, and the village burned. She was one of the few survivors of the attack, and on the smoking ruins of the temple, she swore her life and sword arm to Sarenrae, promising to protect those who could not protect themselves and to use her power to slay those who would cause harm to the innocent. She had travelled far since becoming a priestess and became a travelling companion to Ezren before the others had joined them.

Merisiel is the only elf in the party, as the rest are humans. She grew up as an orphan among a human settlement. While she stayed young as her human companions grew up, Merisiel became a master at stowing away on ships and has called dozens of cities home. She's not the sharpest knife in the drawer, but she makes up for it by being very agile and skilled with small objects, such as daggers and lock picks. She enjoys the company she's with as they give her the opportunity to travel to distant lands, and besides that, Ezren has become somewhat of a father figure to her.

Eustice related his tale of diving into a crypt on his first solo quest and defeating a skeleton king in the process. The rest of the group couldn't determine if he was brave or foolish in undertaking a mission by himself.

As they got closer to their destination, Eustice pointed out Nettlewood, which was just North, Northeast of Lost Coast Road, and he pointed out the general location of Black Fang's dungeon just South of the road they were on.

They then proceeded southward off the road, and when they reached a small glade, they stopped to rest a bit to conserve their strength for what lay ahead.

Chapter 3

After their short rest, the group picked up their gear and headed towards the dungeon up the hill. They could see that the entrance looked more like a cave than a front door to an underground fortress the closer they got to it.

The closer they got to the entrance, the remnants of a battleground. Dead bodies lay about; the earth scorched.

"Do you think this is the group who came before us?" Valeros asked.

"Not sure, but anything's possible," Ezren said.

"Look, goblin," Merisiel said.

"Let us continue, but be watchful," Kyra said.

As they got to their destination, they saw a curtain of thick, green moss hanging over the entrance, hiding whatever lay beyond. Standing in front of the entrance, the group eyed an old, menacing stone statue of a warrior.

Just beyond the mossy curtain, two drunken goblins lurked inside the cave, watching the group approach. They waited with anticipation for the adventurers to get closer to the entrance of the cavern.

"We must prepare ourselves for anything," Kyra said as she drew her scimitar.

"You don't have to say that twice," Valeros said as he drew his longsword.

Upon seeing the two draw their weapons, Eustice drew the longsword he had acquired from the skeleton king's crypt.

With his quarterstaff in hand, Ezren said, "I'm going to look at this statue a bit closer. Come with me, Merisiel."

"Oooo, will there be treasure in it?" Merisiel asked as she got her rapier in her hand.

"I doubt it," Ezren said.

As Ezren examined the statue, he discovered that its features had been melted away by some kind of acid, and it looked older than himself. "This doesn't look good," he said more to himself.

As Ezren and Merisiel were looking at the statue, the rest of the group moved a little closer to the mossy curtain with their weapons in their hands.

Suddenly, without warning, the mossy curtain parted, and a pair of small, green creatures with melon-shaped heads and toothy mouths came charging out, swinging crude swords.

"Goblins!" yelled Valeros.

Howling their battle cries, the pair of goblins charged to attack the group.

Being quick and agile, Merisiel jumped in front of Ezren with her rapier ready, saying, "Stay behind me, wizard."

Kyra sprung to action and swung her scimitar at one of the creatures, but the little guy was nimble and dodged her attack. Eustice stepped in and swung his sword and fell the other goblin, nearly splitting it in half. The remaining goblin, who Kyra tried to strike down, made a lunge at her, striking her badly to where she couldn't perry the blow. Kyra fell back, bleeding from the cut she received.

Ezren took a step to the side of Merisiel and pointed a finger towards the creature and a ray of freezing ice shot out and struck it a glancing blow, but it didn't slow it down.

Valeros swung his sword in a wide arc at the goblin, but the thing jumped out of the way quickly while Merisiel tried to throw one of her daggers at it with her free hand. The goblin caught sight of the flying dagger, swatted it away with its sword, and sent the dagger off to the side.

With what strength Kyra had after being cut, she brought her weapon down on the creature, slicing it deep across its chest and stomach as it knocked the flying dagger out of the way. With a look of surprise, the goblin fell face first onto the ground dead. After she fell the green creature, Kyra knelt on her knees on the ground from her wound, and both Merisiel and Ezren rushed to her aid.

"Stay alert, there could be more," Ezren told both Valeros and Eustice as he checked on Kyra.

"Kyra, are you okay," Merisiel said.

"I should be fine," Kyra said.

"You need to heal yourself before we continue," Ezren told Kyra.

Valeros and Eustice took a stance near the curtain of moss in case other goblins came out.

Calling on the holy might of the goddess Sarenrae, Kyra was able to heal herself fully. "It is done, I am ready to continue," she said.

Merisiel located and quickly retrieved the dagger she had thrown. Then searched the two dead goblins for anything valuable but only found a dead lizard, empty jugs of wine, and four gold pieces. "Well, that wasn't much," she said while tossing the dead lizard and the jug to the side and pocketing the coins.

After Kyra stood up, she and Merisiel joined the group after searching the goblins, then they all continued onward with Valeros and Eustice in the lead, Merisiel in the middle, and Kyra and Ezren bringing up the rear.

Chapter 4

Valeros and Eustice parted the moss curtain and entered the cave, with the rest of the group following behind. The cave was small with a low ceiling, and on the far side of it, they saw a pair of straw mats with a battered treasure chest sitting between them. The further they went, Valeros noticed a passageway off to his left, which led to a pair of stone doors.

As soon as Merisiel saw the chest, she started towards it, but Ezren stopped her, speaking up quickly, "Be careful with that, it could be a mimic."

"A what?" asked Valeros.

"A creature that can mimic any object just to lure you to your doom," Ezren said.

Merisiel, being stopped in her tracks by Ezren, took a step back, saying, "Oh."

"The straw bedding must be where those foul creatures slept, assuming it was safe for them to do so," Kyra said.

Ezren took a step forward to the chest and, reached out with his quarterstaff, and poked at it. The rest of the group had their weapons ready just in case the chest came to life and started attacking.

After poking at the chest, Ezren said, "I believe it's safe now. It would have sprung to life by now."

"Come, let us watch these doors in case something comes through," Valeros told Eustice.

Together, both warriors stood near the passageway,

watching the double-stone doors together.

"You were good back there, we're glad to have you with us," Valeros said.

"I've been in a few fights with goblins before," Eustice said.

Both Ezren and Kyra stepped back to let Merisiel open the chest, and when she tried to open it, she turned to them and said, "It's locked."

"You didn't find a key to it when you picked the dead goblins' bodies, did you?" Ezren asked.

"No, I didn't. But I think I can pick this lock," Merisiel said.

As Merisiel tried to pick the lock on the chest unsuccessfully, Kyra looked through the straw bedding and found a rusted object. Picking it up, she saw that it was an old iron key.

"I believe I found the key to that chest," Kyra said as Merisiel managed to pick the lock on the chest.

"Don't need it now, I got it opened," Merisiel said as she opened the chest. Peering inside, she saw a small sack, a dagger, a small ruby, and a glass vial of orange liquid.

As Kyra and Ezren peered into the chest, Ezren snatched up the glass vial and said, "I think this will be safer with me for now."

As Kyra picked up the dagger, Merisiel shot her a glance, being annoyed that the treasure was being taken. Ezren saw her annoyance and said, "You have plenty of daggers, Merisiel. You can have the rest."

Kyra walked over to Valeros and Eustice, saying, "Would either of you care to have this."

Valeros took the dagger and looked at it, saying, "This is a good dagger. Here, you can have it." He then handed the dagger to Eustice.

Merisiel took the ruby and the small sack, and, looking into it, she saw that it had quite a few coins. Being satisfied, she pocketed both the ruby and the sack with the coins.

After looking around the chamber, Kyra said, "There is nothing more we can do here, we should move on."

With both Valeros and Eustice in the lead, they went up to the double stone doors and opened them to continue their journey deeper into the dungeon.

Chapter 5

As the stone doors swung open, it revealed a room bathed in a shimmering golden radiance like sunlight reflecting off the ocean. The light emanated from a rune-covered fountain in the centre of the room.

As the group entered further into the chamber, they saw a passageway past the fountain, and to their right was a stone door.

The group gathered close to the fountain to look at it and to see where the light was coming from. They saw that the fountain was made of stone and filled with what appeared to be water and tiny runes were carved around the fountain's lip. They couldn't determine the source of the glow emanating from the fountain at all.

"What do you think these runes mean?" Eustice asked to no one in particular.

"I could be able to decipher these runes, give me a moment," Kyra said.

As Kyra was looking over the runes to determine what they said, Valeros scooped some of the water into the palm of his hand. The water glowed for a few seconds before fading out.

In the meantime, Merisiel thought she had heard voices but determined it was just echoes from the chamber walls from the others talking.

"The runes say that anyone who offers gold to Desna, the goddess of fortune, will receive a boon," Kyra said.

"What does that mean?" Valeros asked after drinking the

water from the fountain.

"Why would you do that? It could have been poisoned," Ezren said to Valeros.

"I thought it was just water. It tasted like underground spring water. I'm not going to die, am I?" Valeros said.

"Sometimes I wonder about you," Ezren said.

"Do you think you should drink it while it's still glowing?" Eustice asked. "It could be magical."

"But what about offering gold to the goddess bit," Ezren said.

"Maybe it's like a wishing well, drop a coin in," Merisiel said. Then, as an afterthought, she said, "You know, I thought I heard something earlier when we came in here, but I could have been wrong."

"It could be nothing, but keep your elf ears open for anything," Kyra said. "Now, who will be the first to test this out."

"Test what out?" Valeros asked.

"Tossing a coin into the fountain and drinking the water while it's still glowing," Ezren said.

They all looked at each other for a moment then Valeros said, "I'll do it, I'll go first."

As Valeros was fishing out a gold coin to toss into the fountain, Merisiel ears perked up. She turned to face the passageway leading out of the chamber behind her.

Valeros dropped the coin into the fountain, then scooped up some of the water and drank it while it was still glowing. The others looked at him while Merisiel was watching the passage.

"Well?" Ezren asked.

"Nothing," Valeros said.

Ezren thought about it for a moment, then decided to drop a coin in and drink the glowing water. He then felt a surge of energy course through him, making his reflexes and his mind better than before. He then said, "I feel stronger, better reflexes, and sound mind. I believe it does work."

As Eustice was getting a coin out to drop into the fountain, Kyra went to Merisiel and whispered, "Merisiel, what's wrong."

"I hear voices coming from that passage. It sounds like goblins are arguing with each other, but I don't know what they're arguing about," Merisiel whispered back.

When Eustice drank the glowing water, he, too, felt a change to his body as well.

Kyra turned to the others and said, "There are more goblins down that way." She was pointing towards the passageway then said, "I think it's best we go through that door and see what's beyond it. I don't feel like encountering any more of those foul creatures right now."

"Well then, let's proceed. I believe there is nothing else here for us to do. Valeros, Eustice, lead on," Ezren said.

With that, Valeros and Eustice took up the lead, with Merisiel in the middle and Ezren and Kyra bringing up the rear. With weapons in hand, Valeros opened the door to the next chamber.

Chapter 6

As Valeros opened the door, it silently swung open, revealing a chamber bathed in red light. On the other side of the room, a pair of stone statues stood on either side of a dusty altar that was inscribed with runes. Atop the altar sat a large red gemstone, which the creepy red light came from it. Off to their right, a few feet away, is another stone door that was closed.

As the group entered the chamber, a loud booming voice rang out, saying, "Approach with humility and live!"

As they stopped in their tracks, Merisiel asked, "What does that supposed to mean?"

"I'm not sure, but it does mean something. Let me ponder on this," Kyra said.

"That's a nice gemstone," Merisiel said as she eyed the glowing red gemstone that was on the altar.

Ezren put a hand on Merisiel's arm to keep her back and said, "Somethings not right here. Why would they have that gemstone out in the open, unguarded or unprotected like that? I advise no one goes near it."

"It could be a trap," Eustice said.

Merisiel scanned the floor and the surrounding area to find anything out of place but couldn't find anything. Ezren, meanwhile, focused his magical energy throughout the room for a moment. As he was casting his magick, Kyra said, "I believe I know what it meant by approaching with humility. Approaching a goddess or a god with humility, you must kneel before them."

"So, what you're saying is that you must crawl to that altar," Valeros said.

"If you want to live, yes," Kyra said.

They looked back at the gemstone, and as they looked over at the statues in curious wonderment, Ezren said, "Those statues and that gemstone are magical. I think if anyone gets too close to that gemstone, something bad happens."

"So, what do we do?" Eustice asked.

"Well, if we want that gemstone, one of us has to crawl over there while the rest of us stay far away from harm," Valeros said.

Unbeknownst to them, Merisiel got down on her hands and knees and started crawling towards the altar while the others discussed the next plan of action.

"Where is Merisiel?" Kyra asked while looking over the rest of the group.

Ezren turned to look towards the altar and saw Merisiel crawling ever closer to it. "Merisiel, wait, no!" Ezren shouted.

Then everything happened all at once.

"Get out!" Valeros shouted while snatching Kyra and shoving her through the opened doorway, they came through. Eustice flattened himself against the wall near the doorway that Kyra was shoved through, and Ezren threw himself onto the floor. Just as Merisiel was a few feet from the altar, the statues emitted a cone-shaped fan of flames above her head, filling the chamber with fire.

The flames didn't touch Eustice or Ezren, but they felt the heat. It lasted a few seconds, and within that time, Merisiel managed to grab the gemstone, burning her hand in the process, causing her to yelp in pain. She then quickly crawled back to the group.

They all waited for a second burst of flames to shoot out of the statues for a few seconds, and when none did, they gathered themselves far away from the altar.

"I got the gemstone, but I burnt myself," Merisiel said while holding it out in her other hand that wasn't burnt.

Ezren snatched the gemstone out of her hand, saying, "Next time, warn us if you're going to do something like that."

"Hey, I'm the one who got it," Merisiel said to Ezren.

"Serves you right for getting burnt, but only on your hand. It could have been a lot worse," Kyra said while inspecting the injury Merisiel received.

"Didn't you hear me when I said this gem is magical? I didn't know what kind yet," Ezren said.

"You'll be fine, your hand isn't burnt too much," Kyra said to Merisiel.

"That was a close call," Eustice said.

"Tell me about it," Valeros said.

Ezren casted his magick on the gem and found out what it really is. "This is very magical indeed. It's called an energy heart. I'll keep it with me for safekeeping," he said.

"So, I did the hard work of getting it, and you're keeping it?" Merisiel asked.

"You nearly killed us," Ezren said.

"Not to change the subject, but where do we go from here?" Valeros asked.

"We should see what's beyond that door," Kyra said, pointing to the closed stone door.

"Right, let's go. But first, we need to light a couple of torches," Ezren said.

Just like before, they went to the door with both warriors in front, Merisiel in the middle, and the wizard and priestess bringing up the rear, staying far away from the altar and statues as possible.

Chapter 7

As Valeros opened the door and stepped through the opening with Eustice, they saw thick webs hanging from the corners and ceiling of the chamber. Dozens of tiny spiders crawled about on the webs, but they were far too small to be the source of the large webs.

"Careful, there are large spider webs on the other side of this chamber. Might want to stick to the wall away from those," Valeros said to the others as the rest of the group entered the room.

"I hate to see the spider that made that," Eustice said.

They all turned left upon entering the chamber, staying near the wall far away from the large webs. As they walked along the wall of the chamber, they kept an eye on the large webs to spot anything out of the ordinary. After a few feet, Merisiel spotted something in the webs.

"What's that?" Merisiel asked, pointing at what she had spotted.

As Eustice brought his torch around for better light, the rest of the group saw a body lying within the webbing not far from them.

"That's a goblin," Valeros said.

"Looks like it's been dead for a few days," Kyra said.

"It might have something on it. I'm gonna check it, watch my back," Merisiel said.

"Be careful," Ezren warned her.

While the others stayed back to keep a lookout, Merisiel went to the dead goblin, and as she got close to it, a giant spider came out of its hiding place and rushed at her, but she saw it in time to jump back and tried to pierce it with her rapier but missed.

The others had no idea what was going on until the spider lunged at Merisiel, biting her, causing severe damage with its poison coursing in her, making her sick.

Kyra was the first to act, yelling, "Merisiel, get out of the way!" Kyra jumped into the fray, swinging her scimitar at the creature, but the thing was too fast for her to strike a blow. Then Ezren fired a blast of magical force at the spider, causing some damage to it.

Eustice sprang into action to help and swung his sword and chopped off one of its legs in the process. Valeros then rushed the spider and, with all his strength, cut the creature in two, dispatching it quickly.

Ezren quickly went to help Merisiel up and got her to the wall far away from the spider webs and sat her down, saying, "Are you okay?"

"I feel a little sick. It must have happened when that thing bit me," Merisiel said.

Speaking over his shoulder, Ezren said to the others, "Check to see if there are any others like that spider you killed, Valeros."

Upon hearing that, Valeros and the others with him started poking into the webbing with their weapons being careful not to get too close to the sticky stuff.

After inspecting her wound, Ezren said, "That's a nasty bite. Here, drink this." Ezren pulled out the glass vial of orange liquid out of his pack and gave it to Merisiel. As she drank the liquid, she started to feel a lot better immediately.

"What was that stuff?" she asked.

"It was a potion of healing. I knew it would come in handy," Ezren said.

Kyra came over to where Ezren and Merisiel were and said, "I don't believe there are any more of those things. How are you doing?"

"I feel better now," Merisiel said.

In the meantime, Valeros and Eustice checked the body of the dead goblin, and after they finished searching the body, they went back to where the others waited. Valeros said, "Look what we found."

Eustice held up a wooden dragon toy, and Valeros held out a wand, and when Ezren spied the wand, he said, "I'm able to use that wand. After all, I am a wizard."

Valeros reluctantly handed the wand over to Ezren, then Merisiel spoke up quickly saying, "Was there anything else?"

"No, there wasn't," Valeros said as his pouch contained a few extra coins from the dead goblin. Merisiel eyed him suspiciously, not really believing what he said.

"You should keep that. It might be worth something," Kyra told Eustice, and with that, he stuck it in his pack for safekeeping.

"We should rest here for a bit before moving on. We all need it," Ezren said.

"That sounds like a good idea," Kyra said.

Chapter 8

After their brief rest, they got up and continued their way further into the dungeon. After walking a few feet, the group came upon an opening to their left and went down a long, cavernous corridor.

In the middle of the corridor near the end of it, they saw a strange stone pillar that was illuminated by the glow of the torch's flames. As they got closer to it, they could see odd symbols and faintly glowing glyphs running up and down the ten-foot-tall obelisk's sides.

Off to their right, it looked like someone used chalk to write on one of the rough stones of the cavern wall. It read, *The goblins fear the wyrm and do not venture through the crypt to its lair. Its breath is death.*

Some feet beyond the pillar, they could hear the faint sound of water lapping the shore of the cavern floor.

While Merisiel, Valeros, and Eustice were looking over the words on the wall, Kyra got out one of her torches and lit it, and she and Ezren went over to the pillar and examined the symbols on it.

"What is a wyrm?" Eustice asked.

"It means dragon," Merisiel said.

"Do you think it's about, *Black Fang*?" Valeros asked.

"I don't know," Eustice said.

"I hope not, that'll be bad," Merisiel said.

Meanwhile, as Ezren and Kyra were looking over the pillar,

Ezren said, "These are arcane symbols. And there is one symbol that is in more than one place."

"Oh, which one is that?" Kyra asked.

"This one," Ezren said, pointing out the symbol.

"What does it mean?" Kyra asked.

"It's the symbol for water," Ezren said.

As Kyra and Ezren stood there pondering for a moment, they could still hear water lapping at the shore of the cavern floor in the silence. With the thought of water on her mind, Kyra turned her head towards the sound of the lapping and then took a few steps further down the corridor before stopping. Ezren followed right behind her and came up beside her. They stood there looking upon a large pool of water dominating a large cavern, and then Kyra blurted out, "Water."

Kyra and Ezren both went back to the pillar and found the rest of the group standing around it.

"What do you think this is for?" Valeros asked.

"Kyra and I believe it has something to do with the body of water back there," Ezren said while pointing back towards the pool of water behind them.

"Really? Well, let's check it out," Merisiel said.

They all went to the edge of the pool, and on the far side of it, Merisiel spotted a small island, which something glittered faintly in the glow of the light from the flames from their torches. Off to their left is a path cutting between the cavern wall and the body of water. Merisiel pointed out the island to the rest of the group, saying, "There is an island over there with something on it."

"Gonna have to swim over there if we want to see what's there," Eustice said.

"So, who's the better swimmer," Kyra said.

"I'm pretty good," Eustice said.

"So am I," Valeros said.

After deep in thought, Ezren spoke up, saying, "Whoever designed that pillar is probably the same one who put whatever on that piece of land over yonder."

"What do you mean?" Merisiel asked.

"There is a symbol meaning water on each side of that pillar," Ezren said.

"So, it's a magical pillar," Kyra said.

"Yes, it may have helped the person get across easily and back," Ezren said.

"So, how does it work?" Valeros asked.

"I'm not sure yet," Ezren said. "Valeros, get yourself ready to swim across, but take your sword with you just in case. Eustice, come with me."

As Valeros got himself ready to swim across the pool of water, Ezren and Eustice went back to the pillar. As they both went around the obelisk looking at the symbols, Eustice asked, "So, do I have to touch the symbol?"

"Believe you do," Ezren said.

"Why don't you touch them?"

"Because I'm not the one swimming across."

"Good point."

As Eustice went around touching the symbols for water, they briefly glowed blue, and he felt something within himself and said, "I believe I can breathe underwater."

"That's great, come, hurry. I don't think it will last long, though. Magick rarely does," Ezren said.

They hurried back to where the others waited at the edge of the pool, and when they got there, Kyra asked, "You two ready?"

"Yes, let's go," Eustice said.

Both Eustice and Valeros went into the water and swam to the small island without any difficulty. As they came out to the water and stepped onto the mall island, a creature suddenly burst out of the water and tried to attack Valeros but missed him, and both warriors heard a loud clack as the creatures' claws snapped at thin air right behind them.

As they both turned and saw the creature, they took out their swords to do battle with it. Valeros stepped up first and swung his sword and damaged the creature severely, nearly killing it, but it fought on. It struck out with both claws, but it only managed to get Valeros with one of the pinchers holding the warrior fast as the other claw fell a bit short of its mark.

Eustice came in with a killing blow to the creature, and just before it collapsed, it nipped Valeros with the claw that missed him.

"What was that thing?" Eustice asked.

As Valeros nudged it with his foot to make sure it was dead, he said, "I do believe it was a Reefclaw. I heard their good eating, but I don't think I want to try it. It could have been a guardian of that treasure of there."

They then went to see what was lying in a small pile on the ground. Valeros picked up the longsword, and Eustice grabbed two vials of potions and a leather sack full of gold coins.

With the items secured, they swam back to where the others waited for their return, and as soon as Valeros and Eustice got on dry land, they showed the others what they found, except for the sack full of coins.

"Let me have those vials for safekeeping; we might need them later," Ezren said.

After looking at the sword, Ezren said, "That sword may be magical, let me find out if it is."

Valeros then handed the sword over to Ezren's hilt first. As Ezren was holding onto the sword, he focused his energy over it for a moment before saying, "Yes, it is magical. It's a dragon-bane sword here; you may need this."

Ezren handed the longsword back to Valeros, and then Ezren said, "You two need to get your gear back on so we can continue our journey."

Valeros and Eustice quickly gathered their equipment, and as soon as they were done, the whole group set out. As they walked the path between the water and the cavern wall, Valeros mentioned that he and Eustice had to fight off a Reefclaw on the small island.

"It must have been the guardian of that treasure," Kyra said.

"I said the same thing," Valeros said.

The path they walked on curved to the right, and before long, they came upon an opening to their left. They went through the opening, entering a small cavern and hearing voices beyond.

"There's goblins up ahead, and it sounds like they're arguing," Eustice said.

"They could be the same ones I heard earlier," Merisiel said.

"Tread carefully," Kyra said.

They slowly made their way into a large, cavernous chamber.

Chapter 9

As the group slowly walked into the large cavern, they saw that the walls were covered with crude drawings of goblins. In the corner to their far left, they saw a throne made from animal bones, with a goblin wearing a crown of bones and feathers sitting on the throne. Four more goblins are nearby the one wearing the crown, arguing violently with each other. The goblin on the throne appeared annoyed, and it was covering his ears as the four other goblins shoved and screamed at each other.

Valeros and Eustice were about to charge the goblins for a surprise attack, but Ezren stopped them and whispered, "Wait, we may be able to talk our way out of this. But be on your guard nonetheless."

As they all entered the cavern further, the arguing goblins stopped and stared at the five intruders. The Chief goblin composed himself immediately, sat up straight, and in a loud voice said, "Who you? This throne room of me, King Fatmouth!"

As Ezren was about to speak, Kyra stepped in front and said, "Your Highness, we are but humble servants from faraway lands on a mission. We only wish to pass through." She then bowed in the Chief goblins' direction.

"Wow, she's good," whispered Merisiel.

King Fatmouth was so pleased by Kyra's response that he sat up straighter and appeared to be more 'noble' in his own way. He then said, "Me sister, Bucktooth, stole a dragon toy. Her missing now. These idiots too scared to go find toy. If you go find toy, Me let you live. And me let you go through throne room as much as you want!"

"A toy dragon?" asked Ezren.

"Yes. Mouth and wings move. Bucktooth went into the cave with spider webs. Never to return," King Fatmouth said.

Ezren turned to Eustice and asked, "Don't you have that little wooden dragon?"

"I do," Eustice said, and he fished the wooden dragon out of his pack and handed it to Kyra.

"I believe this is the item you seek. I am sorry, but Bucktooth was killed by a giant spider some time ago," Kyra said as she handed the wooden dragon over to King Fatmouth.

The four goblins shrieked with delight at the return of the toy. Being happy that his minions aren't fighting any more, King Fatmouth said, "If you here to fight a dragon, aim for the belly. Got soft belly scales. Its lair is up there," the goblin Chief pointed up at a cliff leading up to an opening behind the five adventurers. He then fished through his treasure, produced a golden ring, and handed it to Kyra.

Kyra bowed to King Fatmouth and said, "Your Highness, it's been a pleasure." She then returned to the others and led them to the cliff that led to the entrance to another chamber.

Chapter 10

As they were at the cliff face, Kyra was holding out the golden ring and inspecting it.

"He gave that to you?" Merisiel asked.

"Yes, but there is something odd about it, though," Kyra said. She closed her eyes and prayed a little, and when she opened her eyes, she said, "This is a ring of protection. Here, Ezren, you may need it more than the rest of us."

Ezren accepted the ring from Kyra and put it on his finger, feeling the power course through him.

Eustice looked up the cliff wall and noticed there was no rope hanging down and asked, "How are we supposed to get up there?"

The rest of the group looked up, pondering the situation then Ezren said, "One of us could levitate up there."

"How are we to do that? If you noticed, we don't have wings," Valeros said.

"Remember the potions you brought back from that island. One of them is a levitation potion," Ezren said.

"Which one of us will use it to get up there?" Kyra asked.

"I'll do it. I'm lighter than any of you," Merisiel said.

"Are you sure," Ezren said.

"I'm sure," Merisiel said.

Ezren got out the vials, looked at them, and then handed one of them to Merisiel, saying, "This is the one."

Merisiel uncorked the vial and drank the contents, and she

then floated twenty feet up off the ground. She was standing at the top of the cliff wall while the rest of the group watched. She got to the top landing of the cliff and steadied herself, and once there, she noticed a piton that was hammered into the floor and a rope tied to it.

Somebody must have been up here before, she thought to herself as she took the rope and flung it over the side of the cliff, making sure the other end was tied tight to the piton.

The other end of the rope reached the others, and as it did, Valeros grabbed at it quickly and tried to climb up, but in his hasty attempt at climbing, he slipped and fell on his back. "Ouch," he yelped upon landing hard on the ground.

"Are you hurt?" Kyra asked sarcastically.

"Just my pride," Valeros said as he got back up on his feet.

"Be careful next time. Take it slow," Ezren said.

Valeros grabbed hold of the rope again and climbed it to the top, landing, and meeting Merisiel, and one by one, the remaining climbed the rope to the top of the cliff after Valeros.

"Has someone been up here before, or did you do this," Kyra asked Merisiel, indicating the rope and piton.

"I didn't do that. It was there when I got up here," Merisiel said.

They looked about the chamber, and it looked like it was once a sort of ceremonial burial chamber, but now it's just a ruin with bones and cobwebs littering the place. A gentle wind blew through, carrying with it a faint sound of something shuffling in the darkness up ahead.

"There is something in here with us," Kyra said.

"Let's proceed with caution," Ezren said.

They hadn't gone far when Valeros spotted three shambling skeletons ahead of them in the chamber.

"Crikey, their skeletons, the undead," Valeros said.

Upon seeing Valeros and Eustice, who were in the lead, the humanoid skeletons started to shamble to the group to attack. Kyra stepped up quickly and channelled her energy, creating a burst of divine power against the undead skeletons. Two of them were destroyed immediately, but the third was still intact and kept moving towards the group. Ezren then stepped into combat and swung his quarterstaff at the remaining skeleton but missed it entirely, nearly hitting Valeros with it.

"Watch where you swing that thing," Valeros said.

"Sorry," Ezren said.

As Merisiel struck the thing with her rapier, it seemed like her weapon only went between the skeleton's rib cage, not doing any damage. The remaining skeleton swiped at Valeros with its clawed hand, but Valero sidestepped out of the way, avoiding the thing's attack, and he swung his newly acquired longsword while doing so, shattering the undead creature, sending the bones everywhere.

"That was a close call," Valeros said.

"Is this some sort of crypt?" Eustice asked as he looked around his surroundings.

"I believe it is," Kyra said.

"This isn't good," Merisiel said.

"Why do you say that?" Ezren asked.

"There is a dragon's lair beyond this chamber," Valeros said.

"How do you know that?" Kyra asked.

"There is writing on the wall where that pillar is saying that the goblins fear the wyrm, and they don't venture through the crypt to its lair," Merisiel said.

"So, we must continue to the end then," Kyra said.

"The goddess Sarenrae must be with us this day," Eustice

said.

"She's with me always," Kyra said as they continued down the chamber, keeping a watchful eye out for any more of the undead.

When they got to the end of the passage, the group turned right and walked down a short hallway before having to make another right, and they came upon a set of stairs leading down. There, at the top of the stairs, they stopped before descending the staircase to discuss their battle plans.

Chapter 11

The winding passageway the group took ended at a staircase in the back of an ancient warren set inside the hillside. Just before the opening that led to the top landing of the stairs, they stopped and huddled together to discuss their plans. The chamber beyond opened to the sky above and the crumbling ruin was littered with debris.

"How are we going to do this," Kyra asked.

"One of us has to strike it unseen," Ezren said.

"And how are we supposed to do that?" Valeros asked.

"By being invisible," Ezren said.

"That'll be a little hard to do. You're the only wizard here," Merisiel said.

"By drinking this," Ezren said as he produced a vial out of his pack.

"That's one of the potions Valeros and I got off that small island," Eustice said.

"Yes, and believe that you, Valeros, should take this as you have the dragon-bane sword," Ezren said.

"I got a bad feeling about this," Valeros said.

"It'll be fine. We'll be right behind you," Kyra said.

"We got your back," Merisiel said.

"What are the rest of you going to do?" Valeros asked.

"I have my crossbow, Kyra her sling, Merisiel her daggers, and Eustice, you flank the creature on your right while Valeros goes on his left," Ezren said.

"Sounds like a good plan," Kyra said.

"Everybody ready," Ezren said.

They all nodded, indicating that they were.

"Just a warning, when you strike the creature, you will be visible to all," Ezren told Valeros.

Valeros drank the potion, and before the group's eyes, he disappeared. He went through the opening and descended the stairs while the rest waited a bit before following.

On the far side of the chamber, they saw a pile of glittering gold and sparkling trinkets piled up to a sizable hoard. The view of the treasure was suddenly obscured as a terrible winged black dragon swooped into view. As it snarls, its black fangs dripped with green acid that burned the floor wherever it landed.

Valeros quickly went up to the dragon and struck it. His newly acquired sword cut deep into the dragon, surprising it. After his strike, Valeros was visible to all, even the black dragon.

Merisiel, being quick and agile, went down the stairs ahead of the rest and flung one of her daggers at the dragon's underbelly, and it sank into its thick hide, causing some damage to the creature.

In pain and highly frustrated that these inferior humanoids would dare to attack it, Black Fang roared and then emitted a stream of green acid out its mouth wildly at the intruders. Merisiel wasn't very lucky as some of the acid had gotten on her, eating some of her exposed skin and clothing. Eustice ran up to Merisiel and got her out of the conflict after he saw what had happened, while Ezren came down the stairs firing his crossbow at the creature, but the bolt missed its mark, and it glanced off one of its hard scales.

As Valeros swung his blade again, the dragon quickly moved out of the way, but it felt a soft thud as a stone bullet struck the creature. The dragon then turned its head to see where the missile came from and saw Kyra by the staircase, getting another stone bullet out to use against the creature.

Merisiel attempted to throw another dagger at the dragon, but being in pain from the acid, the dagger bounced harmlessly off one of the scales of the creature.

Unconcerned with the others except for the immediate threat next to it, Black Fang turned its head towards Valeros and snapped at him with its powerful jaw, but Valeros quickly dodged its attack as the thing's mouth bit empty air. Then, the dragon spread its wings and flew out of the chamber through the opening high above, leaving behind its treasure hoard.

The group watched it fly off in dismay, and then Valeros turned and saw Eustice near Merisiel and said, "I thought you were going to help me."

"Merisiel got burnt by acid. I had to get her out of the way," Eustice said.

Upon seeing how badly injured Merisiel is, Valeros said, "Oh, are you okay?"

"I think so. It kind of hurts," she said.

"We drove it away. I don't think it's coming back. I believe we were too much for it," Ezren said.

"It wasn't fully grown. It was young and brash but very dangerous still," Kyra said. "Don't worry, Merisiel, we'll get you taken care of."

"Thank you, Eustice, for protecting me. Now let's see what it left behind," Merisiel said.

The rest agreed with Merisiel and went to see what the dragon had left behind. What they saw among the pile of gold coins was a shield, half-plate armour, a vial of potion, and two scrolls.

"I'll take those scrolls and the potion for safekeeping. Kyra, you might want to check that shield. It could be magical," Ezren said.

"What about this armour," Valeros said.

"There is no aura coming from it," Kyra said as she laid her hands on the shield.

"I guess you could take the armour," Valeros said to Eustice. "Merisiel, let's divide these coins."

As the group was gathering the items, Kyra said, "This shield is magical, and it's light steel. Which one of you will take it?"

Eustice and Valeros looked at one another, and then they looked at Kyra for a moment before Eustice said, "I believe you should take it, Valeros."

After they had gathered all the treasure, it was an agreement that they should head back the way they had come.

Chapter 12

They went back up the stairs and retraced their steps through the ruined ceremonial burial chambers. When they got to the cliff, they climbed down using the rope that was still tied to the piton to King Fatmouth's throne room.

As soon as they all got down the cliff, Kyra approached the Chief goblin and told him that they had driven the dragon away. Upon hearing the news, King Fatmouth and the other goblins cheered, and King Fatmouth proclaimed that the adventurers were friends of his tribe and that the group, at any time, could come to his domain without fear of being attacked, and they could rest there.

Kyra and the others thanked him, and the brave heroes left out of the caverns. On their way to Sandpoint, while on Lost Coast Road, the group kept an eye on the sky in case they ran across Black Fang. They had met a few travellers on the road who said they saw something in the sky going westward but had disappeared.

When they reached Sandpoint, the group sought an audience with the mayor, Kendra Deverin. Kyra and Ezren told her what the party had done and told her that they were not able to kill the dragon but were able to drive it away.

Kendra thanked the heroes for their efforts and bid them to stay for a feast in their honour, which was held the next day.

For two days after the feast, they stayed at the Rusty Dragon to rest and plot their next adventure.